SUPER ROOSTER SAVES the DAY

BY MAUREEN WRIGHT
ILLUSTRATED BY ROB McCLURKAN

two lions

DEDICATED WITH MUCH LOVE
TO MY GRANDSON,
NATHANAEL WRIGHT
—M.W.

FOR MY NIECES,
MIRANDA AND ANNALEE
—R.M.

Published by Two Lions, New York
www.apub.com
Amazon, the Amazon logo, and Two Lions are trademarks of Amazon.com, Inc., or its affiliates.

ISBN-13: 9781542007788
ISBN-10: 154200778X

The illustrations are rendered in digital media.
Book design by Liz Casal

Printed in China
First Edition
10 9 8 7 6 5 4 3 2 1

Ralph the rooster
always wanted to be a superhero.

He could **crow** and make the sun rise...but only when it wasn't raining.

He had his very own **cape**... when the farmer wasn't using it.

He could **fly**... for short distances.

He could make himself **invisible**...if he pretended he was a weather vane.

But he didn't fool the other animals.

"Stop kiddin' around," grumbled George. "We know you're just plain old Ralph the rooster."

"He's udderly ridiculous," mooed Caroline.

"You're not pulling the wool over my eyes," said Sheila.

Ralph did have one friend on the farm who believed in him.

"Every superhero needs a sidekick!"

oinked Rosie. "And that's me!"

"We're best friends forever," said Ralph.

Deep down, Ralph knew that real superheroes
have super-duper powers and always save the day.
Ralph didn't have powers, and his days were filled with

boring

bird

things.

"I'll never get a chance to be a **real** superhero," sighed Ralph, flopping down in the dirt.

"**Yes, you will,**" said Rosie, rooting in the mud. "**I know you can do it!**"

Then one sunny autumn morning
the farmer left the radio on in the barn.
And everything changed when Ralph heard…

THE CHICKEN DANCE!

Ralph's tail feathers sprang up in the air. The comb on his head shot straight up. Ralph boogied to the beat....

Cheep-cheep-cheep!

Flap-flap-flap!

Wiggle-wiggle-wiggle,

and a clap-clap-clap!

Super-duper powers surged through him. "I can leap off the barn roof in a single bound! I can fly faster than a speeding pullet!" said Ralph.

"What's a pullet?" asked Rosie.

"A young hen," said Ralph.

"That dance is your **super-duper rooster booster!**"
rooted Rosie.

"**Let's go save the day!**"
said Ralph.

Ralph strutted down the lane with Rosie.
"Look!" he said. "That tree is on fire!"

"Time for your
**super-duper
rooster booster!**"
cheered Rosie.

Ralph boogied....

"UnBULLievable!" mooed Caroline. "What are you doing?"

"Putting out the fire," Ralph explained.

"There's no fire," said Caroline. "It's **autumn**. The leaves on the trees turn red, orange, and yellow in the fall."

"Oh," said Ralph. "Well, it's a good thing I watered that tree to help it grow."

"He's the **silliest superhero** I've ever met," muttered George.

"I still believe in you!" rooted Rosie.

Ralph and Rosie searched for a different chance to save the world.

"Look!" said Ralph. "Those geese are flying SOUTH for the winter. They're all confused. They should be flying NORTH."

"Time for your **super-duper rooster booster!**" cheered Rosie.

Ralph boogied.... **Cheep-cheep-cheep! Flap-flap-flap! Wiggle-wiggle-wiggle, and a clap-clap-clap!**

Ralph zoomed into the sky and took over as lead bird.
"COCK-A-DOODLE-DOO!" he crowed.

"HONK! HONK!" said the geese.

POW! WOW!

But Ralph didn't listen. He left the geese flying north and headed back to the farm.

"You just led them the WRONG way," Sheila scolded. "They're supposed to go SOUTH for the winter, where it's warmer."

"Oh," said Ralph. "Well, at least they'll see the pretty fall leaves before they go."

"He doesn't listen to a word we say," complained George.

"In one ear and out the udder," muttered Caroline.

"Don't give up, Ralph!" rooted Rosie.

Ralph and Rosie searched for a different chance to save the world.

As they headed down the lane, hard green baseballs broke off from a tree and dropped to the ground.

SNAP!

THUD!

"**That's dangerous!**" said Ralph. "Someone could get bonked on the head."

"Time for your **super-duper rooster booster!**" cheered Rosie.

Ralph boogied....

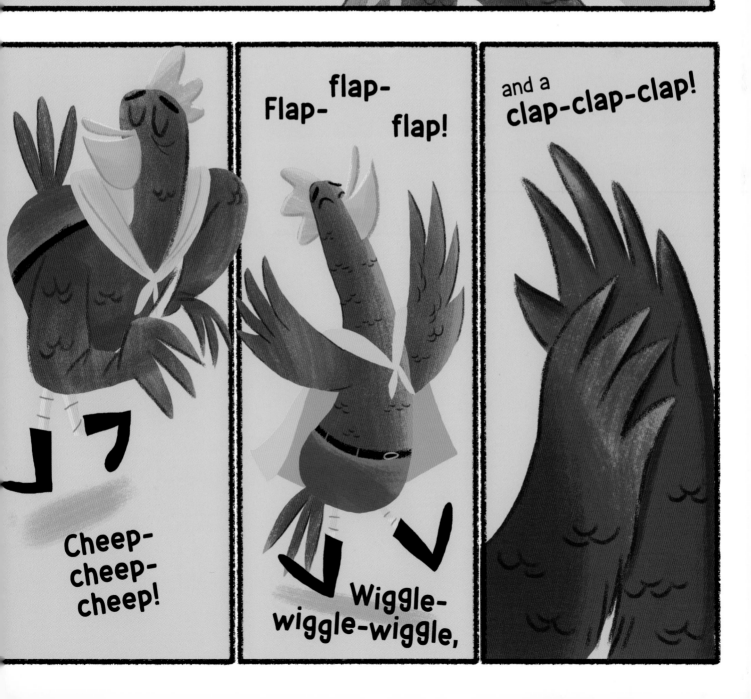

Cheep-cheep-cheep!

Flap- flap- flap!

Wiggle-wiggle-wiggle,

and a clap-clap-clap!

Super-duper powers surged through him. He grabbed a baseball bat and walloped each ball high into the sky.

POW!
WOW!

"Swing-batter-batter-swing!"
called Rosie.

"What are you doing now?" asked George.

"Getting rid of these baseballs," said Ralph.

"Baaaaad moooove," said Sheila and Caroline together.

"They're not baseballs; they're walnuts," explained George.

"See the nut inside the shell? Squirrels love to eat walnuts. They save them for winter."

"Oh," said Ralph. "Well, it's a good thing I shared those walnuts with the hungry squirrels who live far away from here."

"Hey! I'm getting hungry!" said Rosie.
"Let's eat some corn!" said Ralph.

But when they arrived at the cornfield...

...crows were gobbling up all the corn!

"Oh no!" cried Ralph. "There won't be any left if we don't stop them!"

Ralph boogied.... **Cheep-cheep-cheep!**
Flap-flap-flap! Wiggle-wiggle-wiggle,
and a **clap-clap-clap!**

POW! WOW!

Ralph zoomed around the cornfield,
but there were just too many crows
to chase away.

The other animals ran to the field
to see what was happening.

"Look…up in the sky!" shouted Sheila.
"What is that?"

George said, "It's a bird! It's a plane!
No, wait, it really IS a bird!"

"It's RALPH!" cried Caroline. "He's trying
to save the corn! We need to help him!"

"Everyone do the chicken dance!" yelled Rosie.

The animals boogied....

Cheep-cheep-cheep!

Flap-flap-flap!

The crows were shocked to see the dancing animals!

Wiggle-wiggle-wiggle,

and a **clap-clap-clap!**

ZIP!

Ralph darted and dived
as crows flap-flap-flapped
their wings in fright and
flew away.

SWOOSH!

ZOOM!

"Hooray!" hollered George.

"A-m-m-m-mazing!" mooed Caroline.

"Now that's something to crow about!" said Sheila.

"COCK-A-DOODLE-DOO!" crowed Ralph.

"I couldn't have done it without you, and especially Rosie, the best friend a hero ever had!"

That night they had a dance party in the barn.

"Three cheers for Ralph the Super Rooster!" they whooped and hollered. "Once in a while, he really does save the day!"